Arjun The One

AF080798

OrangeBooks Publication

1st Floor, Rajhans Arcade, Mall Road, Kohka, Bhilai, Chhattisgarh 490020

Website:**www.orangebooks.in**

© Copyright, 2024, Author

All rights reserved. No part of this book may be reproduced, stored in a retrieval system, or transmitted, in any form by any means, electronic, mechanical, magnetic, optical, chemical, manual, photocopying, recording or otherwise, without the prior written consent of its writer.

First Edition, 2024

ISBN: 978-93-5621-768-3

ARJUN THE ONE

Shankar S Kurup

OrangeBooks Publication
www.orangebooks.in

Content

Chapter — One 1
   The Beginning 2

Chapter — Two 9
   Meet Maya 10

Chapter — Three 19
   Digging The Past 20

Chapter — Four 33
   Mission Here We Come 34

Chapter — Five 47
   The Final Showdown............................ 48

Chapter – One

The Beginning

Vishnu and his wife Anjali stayed at Trivandrum, which lies in the southern part of India, with their two sons. Their elder son, Arjun, was pursuing engineering in a reputed college in Trivandrum and the younger one, Abhimanyu, was in 10th grade CBSE, and was on study leave waiting for the exams in a couple of days. Arjun always excelled in his studies as he had been good at time management ever since he was a child. Both children were die-hard fans of cricket; their interest was inherited from their father, for which their mother, Anjali, was not in much favour. She always insisted her children do nothing but study! Abhimanyu was lost in curiously watching an intense high-voltage World Cup cricket match between the arch-rivals, India and Pakistan. He heard a scream, "ABHI......!" from his mom.

"Why are you wasting time like this? It's better go to your room and study. Don't you know that only a couple of days are remaining for your board exams?" She finished her line.

"But Mom... I was studying the whole day and finished my portions to watch this match. This is India Vs Pakistan, the mother of all matches. Anyway, this will get over in half an hour, and we are winning too!" replied Abhimanyu in one breath without taking eyes from the TV.

"Alright, after all it is your call; if you do not fare well in the exams, there will be a heated match between us when your result comes," said Anjali, locking her eyes on Abhimanyu.

They were interrupted by a knock at the door, followed by Vishnu's voice, "It is me." Anjali opened the door; Vishnu and Arjun entered.

"Arjun, how come you came so early? Your tuition is supposed to be till 9:30," asked Anjali sounding surprised.

"Dad pulled me out of tuition." said Arjun with a smile as his eyes glued to the TV.

Vishnu smelt trouble, seeing Anjali turning towards him.

"Ha ha ha, don't be angry, dear," said Vishnu winking at Arjun to support him to get out of this crisis.

"Yes, Mom," said Arjun. Vishnu turned towards Arjun as if to say,

'Is that all you have to say?' "You both need not defend each other," said Anjali, staring at them.

"Look Anjali," said Vishnu in an attempt to finish this discussion so that they can focus on the match, "This is the 50 over World Cup, which only happens once in 4 years, and today, it is between India and Pakistan, where India is winning, so it is more interesting to watch!"

"But, why did you pull him from the tuition?" Anjali was not ready to leave the subject.

"All I wanted was to watch the match together with family, so please don't get over dramatic and spoil the mood. Arjun goes to tuition thrice a week; a skip of half an hour today won't change anything. You also know that both our kids are responsible and good at their studies; moreover, they know very well how to manage their time properly and finish their portions as per their schedule," said Vishnu, tilting his head between the TV and Anjali.

"You are right, dad," confirmed Arjun without turning away from the TV. "Today's attendance was very lean, so the teacher didn't take any new lesson and was planning to leave us early."

"All right then," said Anjali in a low voice.

"Now, you come and sit here, let us all watch together and cheer for our team. We have bought food from the hotel for tonight. Somebody, bring Ricky in. Let him also enjoy our company," said Vishnu, referring to their pet dog.

"Ok, I shall get the food and serve; Abhi, you go and bring Ricky in," said Anjali.

"Right-on, Mom" said Abhimanyu, leaving the room quickly and came back with Ricky in no time! They all cheered as India won the match, and Ricky sitting on the couch, wagged his tail.

After a couple of days, Abhimanyu seemed to be little bit nervous and tensed as he was going to experience his board exams for the first time.

He woke up early and started revising again. Anjali was busy in the pooja room praying for her son to do well in the exam. Vishnu reminded him to take all the necessary items required for the exam.

Vishnu said, "Abhi, it is time to leave; hurry up."

"Ok dad," replied Abhimanyu with tension in his voice.

On hearing Abhimanyu murmured something to himself as if he had forgotten to keep something in his bag,

Arjun came to him and asked "Hey Abhi, what is the matter? Do you want me to help you?"

"Thanks, at last, I got my hall ticket, which I misplaced." Abhimanyu answered in relief.

Arjun patted Abhimanyu and said, "See Abhi, you do not get tensed or nervous, or else you may forget whatever you have studied. I am sure that you will do awesome as you prepared well. Be confident, good luck bro." then he handed over his calculator and said, "Keep this you can use this and I hope you have not forgotten your geometry box?"

"No, I kept my geometry box in my bag. Thanks brother." Abhimanyu replied.

"Ok Abhi, you better get going, else dad may pounce on you for the delay!" said Arjun with a smile.

"Yes, you are right. I am leaving," said Abhimanyu. As he was about to leave, Anjali applied Vibhuthi on Abhimanyu's forehead, hugged him and emotionally said, "Do your best, Abhi."

"Don't be emotional, Anjali. Our son will clear this exam with flying colors. You need not worry." Vishnu said turning towards Abhimayu and asking, "What do you say, Abhi?"

"Certainly, dad," replied Abhimanyu with confidence, who is now motivated by his dad's word. "All the best, my son. Good luck, take care," wished Vishnu.

"Thanks Dad," said Abhimanyu and took blessings from dad, mom and brother. He waved at them; they all waved him back as he left for school in his bicycle.

In a jiffy, weeks passed by, and Abhimanyu's exams got over. He came back from school threw his bag in his room and ran out of his house.

Anjali who noticed this, shouted, "Abhi, stop right there. At least tell me how the exam was and then leave."

"Today's paper was very good. I wrote it really well like all the other subjects, mom," replied Abhimanyu and ran away in excitement along with Ricky.

"Then, have your snacks and go," said Anjali. She looked for Abhimanyu, but he was nowhere in the vicinity as if he had vanished!

"This kid!" said Anjali in anger.

All his friends are in the state syllabus and finished their final exams a week ago. On the way to the ground with his cycle and Ricky, he thought of the state of mind he was in a week ago when all his friends in the neighborhood, after finishing their exam, knocked on his door, asking to play with them and he would feel sad and reply, "Sorry, guys. exams!!... And please don't knock on my door till my exam is over" and he would close the door with a frown face.

Finally, he reached the ground. On reaching the ground, he saw that all his friends were playing their favorite game, cricket. One of his friends, Dhruv, was bowling to another friend, Rishi. Dhruv noticed Abhimanyu and yelled, "Oh, look guys, its Abhi!!!".

All his friends came running towards him except Rishi, who stood there in his crease in shock because he needed only two runs to win the match.

"Guys, wait! I am about to win. Why are you running towards Abhi??? Let's finish the match!!!"

"Come on, Rishi; Abhi has come to play after weeks," replied Dhruv. After chatting for 5 to 10 minutes, Abhimanyu said, "Let's play!!'

All the boys ran towards the wicket, picked the team and started to play. As the match progressed, Abhi was batting; his team needed fifteen runs to win the match in two overs. Abhi was his team's star batsman. Rishi came running with all his might and bowled a delivery, to which Abhimanyu flung his bat as hard as he could; the ball flew past the street and ended up landing inside the "haunted house" infested with bats, spider webs and told to be the house of ghosts!!! All the other kids ran away back home except Rishi, Dhruv and Abhimanyu, who ran to the gate of the haunted house. Ricky barked more aggressively than usual as if he sensed the presence of a spirit.

"You take the ball; it is the second ball that has landed inside the haunted house," demanded Rishi to Abhimanyu.

"Why should I?" was his reply.

"You hit it, right?" said Dhruv

"You bowled it, right? We lost another ball the last time we played, but that is just next to the main door of the haunted house," replied Abhimanyu in defence.

"So... Nobody here is brave enough to jump in?" Quizzed Dhruv.

At this moment, Arjun was heading towards home, passing the "haunted house" in his Black Fazer. As he heard the chit-chat of the ball, Arjun went up to the boys and said, "If the ball is in the house, I will bring it for you!" The boys looked frightened.

Abhimanyu replied, "No brother, both balls are inside the haunted house; one is next to the main door, and the other is inside the house. There is no way we can get that ball which is inside because the main door is locked from outside, and it is getting dark. We shall play with the other ball."

Arjun who was a tough guy didn't heed to the "ghost" scare. "Let me just go and get the ball that is next to the main door, hold this," said Arjun, sounding confident as he handed his bag to Abhimanyu.

"But it is dangerous," said Abhimanyu.

"Don't worry, there is no such thing as ghost; it is just an imagination of people," replied Arjun as he jumped the wall attached to the rusted and closed gate. Watching Arjun running towards the door, Abhimanyu and his friend's held the gate in fear and anticipation, as Ricky kept barking.

"Arjun!!!!" screamed Abhi and his friends. Abhimanyu was the most tense. When Arjun reached the main door of the 'haunted house', he could see the ball lying close to the door. He leaned towards the ball to grab it, when he heard someone murmuring his name, "ARJUN!!!" from inside the locked house.

Before he could react, all of a sudden, the lock of the door unlocked along with the gate on its own, and the door and gate were wide open. Several bats flew away from the haunted house. Arjun and the boys tried to run, but they could not. They felt that someone was pulling them from inside and into the hall of the house; none of them could move a muscle or scream. Abhimanyu and his friends got frightened. Ricky could not bark. The boys could not scream as if their mouths were closed with force by someone. All of a sudden, they saw a blue circle in front of the door that acted like a shield which came out of nowhere… The door closed by itself. Lights were suddenly glowing as though someone had switched the lights on. The house had no furniture. The emptiness was felt in the house. A staircase all the way to the top floor was designed with beauty, old paintings fixed all over the faded-colored walls. Now, the boys could move themselves. They all tried to open the door with all their might but in vain.

Ricky barked as loud as he could as his eyes were locked onto a corner from where suddenly a voice appeared, "No use, you can't open the door!!!"

A blue light was right in front of them. The blue light disappeared, and a young lady appeared out of nowhere. The boys were shocked when the lady appeared.

"WHO ARE YOU???" screamed Arjun in anger; the other boys were right behind Arjun.

Chapter – Two

Shankar S Kurup

Meet Maya

I am Maya!!! Said the lady, who appeared to be a soul levitating off the floor. "What do you want from us?" asked Arjun in a heated voice. The boys were visually very confused as to what was happening. "I want your help!!!" said Maya. Ricky stopped barking after Arjun said, "Ricky hush". Now, Ricky was a spectator who lay down in a corner while never taking his eyes away from Arjun and Abhimanyu. "What??? A soul like you want our help???" asked Arjun in amusement. "Yes, all of you, but mainly, your help, Arjun," replied Maya. "Then why the hell did you bring all the others here???" asked Arjun. "Yes. What's all this about?" questioned Abhimanyu. "Look, kids. My soul needs eternal bliss, which is only possible if you help me," said Maya. "Eternal what???" questioned Dhruv. "Eternal bliss is Moksha, where your soul gets freedom, and it is believed that if your soul attains Moksha, you will be in heaven forever," replied Abhimanyu.

"Oh, ok. But what should we do??? Why did you rope only us in? What do we get to do with your moksha???" asked Dhruv.

"It is a long story," replied Maya.

"Come on, Maya. We are normal kids whose parents get worried if we are not home on time," told Arjun.

"Yeah, and my dad would be waiting for me with a cane by now," said Rishi, sounding concerned.

"Ok. I will let you go now. Since you guys came to me, now, I can create your body double and make that body do anything I want," said Maya.

"Then, why don't you just make that body? Do what you want and leave us," asked Dhruv.

"I can surely make your body double and control it, but I can't get out of here. My soul is trapped here until my mission is complete. Furthermore, I can control your body for a limited period of time only if you are connected to me with the ring, and the body should be here in Lakshya at the time I make the body double and... Arjun is the chosen one." explained Maya.

"Chosen one???" questioned Arjun.

"You are the chosen one. Our souls have a history, Arjun. Each one of you has a connection to each other from your past birth. You guys were together in your past life, too. Arjun is the brave one, Abhimanyu is the think-tank, Dhruv is the one with strength, and Rishi is the one with extrovert qualities in him, which makes your circle the best for my mission or our mission. Since our souls have a connection from the past, only you guys can complete the mission," said Maya.

"You have still not told us the story as to why we are the ones to complete your mission. If all four are in this together, how come I am the chosen one?" asked Arjun.

"You are their leader, Arjun, and we were in love in our past birth. So, you have a special connection with me. It is you who had the ring when you died in your last birth, which makes it clear that only you can find the magical ring, Arjun. You guys were destined to meet," said Maya "Ring??? What ring?" questioned Arjun.

"All in good times, my friend. I shall brief you about our past story tomorrow since it is our 50th death anniversary. We were all killed on the same day because of the ring," said Maya.

"OH, GOD! What a thrilling experience this is," added Abhimanyu.

"OK! Since it's late, you guy's better head home. We shall meet tomorrow and don't tell anybody about this supernatural experience," warned Maya.

"Why is that?" questioned Dhruv.

"Wow, Sherlock. Who shall believe us if we tell about this story?" Abhimanyu said in a loud tone.

"That is true, and only you four can see me; since you guys have a gist about our mission, you guys can't hold back. You must finish this mission. The reason being we all were killed for a common cause last birth, we must finish what we left off in our last birth, or else...." Maya suddenly looked at the boys and stopped.

"OR ELSE???" Arjun questioned in a concerned tone.

"Sorry to say this, but the ring has a curse that if you guys don't find the ring, you guys will be killed at the same age as your last birth," added Maya.

"WHAT???!!!" screamed all the boys except Arjun. "What age did we die last birth???" asked Dhruv in panic.

"Twenty-two. We were all the same age last birth," added Maya. "That's so young to die!!!" said a shocked Dhruv.

"I don't want to die so early," said Rishi sounding emotional.

"No one wants to die, but if we are destined to complete this mission, then we will do it," said a determined Arjun.

"OK," said the boys in chorus.

"Glad to hear that," added Maya.

"Let me ask you one thing, Maya," interrupted Arjun.

"If we were all killed in our last birth for the ring why you are the only one as a soul???"

"That is because my dad was the one who killed us all in our last birth. He wanted the ring, which I said was with you. The ring with you was a secret, which I exposed to my dad by mistake. It is a curse for my wrong doing. Let's discuss everything in detail tomorrow," said Maya.

"Ok," said the boy, visibly stunned as to what was happening with their lives.

They walked along with Ricky out of the haunted house with thoughts running through them. The gates were open, and as they walked out of the gate, the gates closed. The doors of the haunted house closed, too. Arjun got on his bike as Abhimanyu held Ricky who sat between them. The other two boys were in a spot of shock, as they spoke about the unbelievable experience. Rishi and Dhruv both knew that they were in for a storm at home since it was past their allotted time to reach home. They could only walk slowly due to the magical event that they went through.

"Can you believe what just happened???" Rishi questioned.

"Of course not!!!" answered Dhruv, as he was just staring at a tree far away, lost in thought.

"Me too, my body is still in goosebump mode," said Dhruv. Suddenly, Rishi pinched Dhruv on his arm.

"Hey... Why did you do that???" Asked a confused Dhruv.

"I wanted to know if this was a dream," said Rishi, defending himself.

"If you want to know if it is a dream, you need to pinch yourself, not anyone else," said Dhruv as he pinched Rishi.

"Ouch!!!" screamed Rishi. Before Rishi could do anything, Dhruv said, "We are in for a treat," as he pointed his hand towards the gate to Rishi's house.

Rishi looked and saw Arjun and Abhimanyu talking to Dhruv's and Rishi's dad. Rishi's dad was a manager at a multinational company, and Dhruv's dad was an accountant. Their moms were housewives, and Rishi and Dhruv didn't have any siblings. A shiver ran through Rishi's and Dhruv's minds.

"They are here," said Abhimanyu.

"Arjun was telling me that you guys were late because you went to Mahadev Uncle's house for tea." said Parth , Dhruv's dad.

"Yes dad," replied Dhruv in relief, like a spanking from dad was avoided.

"We were about to leave home to the ground looking for you both, that was when we saw Arjun and Abhi," said Surya, Rishi's dad.

"Oh. Ok dad," said Rishi with a sigh of relief.

"Ok. Let's go," said Surya. "It is time to enter home, boy," said Parth.

"Ok," said the boys.

"Bye, Uncle," said Arjun and Abhimanyu.

"Bye." Parth and Surya replied.

"Meet you tomorrow," said Abhimanyu, as he waved bye to Dhruv and Rishi.

"Bye Abhi and Arjun," said the boys as they looked at Arjun with 'You saved our lives' expressions. Arjun smiled in return and waved them back. Parth and Surya shook each other's hands and parted to their respective houses with Rishi and Dhruv behind them. Arjun started his bike as Abhimanyu held Ricky who sat between them and went home, which was in the street opposite Rishi's and Dhruv's houses. While Arjun and Abhimanyu reached home, Vishnu was having a conversation with Anjali about the haunted house. Abhimanyu got down from the bike while Ricky jumped from his seat and sat in front of the gate. Abhimanyu opened the gate in shock while Arjun entered the parking area with the bike.

"Why is dad discussing the haunted house???" Questioned Arjun as he parked his bike.

"I don't know, but it seems funny that even dad is in on the haunted house topic all of a sudden," replied Abhimanyu.

"Keep cool and let us get into the conversation," added Arjun.

They entered the hall. "Boys!!!!" shouted Vishnu in excitement. Ricky followed them.

"Yes dad," replied Arjun.

"Dad, you were talking about the haunted house to mom?" Abhimanyu asked as he kept his bat aside.

"Yes Abhi, since the time he came from the office today, he has been just chatting about Lakshya, the haunted house." Anjali replied, sounding tired of listening to Vishnu talking about Lakshya.

"Lakshya is going to be a shopping mall soon. My friend Aarav is going to demolish the house and build a shopping mall," said Vishnu. Abhimanyu looked at Arjun with a tense face. "But Dad, isn't it said to be a haunted house???" asked Arjun slowly as if in panic. "That is just a rumor. Aarav has just come back from the US, and he is planning to settle here with his wife, Akshara and son, Vivaan, so he wants to build a shopping mall for Vivaan. He doesn't believe in ghosts and has given the contract to a foreign company. An American builder will come and demolish Lakshya. You know foreigners; they will laugh at us if we say that Lakshya has a ghost protecting it," concluded Vishnu.

Arjun and Abhimanyu didn't know what to tell or do. They seemed perplexed.

"Ok, dad, let me freshen up," said Arjun.

He pulled Abhimanyu and closed the door of his room quickly as Ricky followed them. "Sure. Abhi, you also freshen up, so let's have dinner," said Anjali.

"Right on, Mom!" shouted Abhimanyu from inside Arjun's room.

"You also take a bath," said Anjali to Vishnu.

"Definitely, let me just keep my phone charging," said Vishnu.

Meanwhile Arjun and Abhimanyu were chatting about Maya and Lakshya.

"Tomorrow, we need to tell Maya about the plan to demolish Lakshya," said Arjun.

"That's right, but why is Aarav Uncle demolishing Lakshya right when we had a conversation with Maya???" Abhimanyu questioned, looking doubtful.

"And how come dad, who never discussed Lakshya, is all of a sudden talking about it? I don't think all these happenings we experienced today are a mere coincidence but are predestined." Arjun added in excitement.

Abhimanyu said, "Anyway, things are getting exciting."

"There is something that is more than what meets the eye, Abhi. Last week, we just considered Lakshya as a random horror house. But now, it looks like our life and Maya's eternal bliss depend on it. We need to know more about the demolition," said Arjun.

"Maya told us that if we fail to succeed in our mission, we will end up dying way too early, and if Lakshya goes down, will Maya still be there as a soul???" Abhimanyu asked as he scratched his head in frustration.

"Maya should answer that, Abhi. Let us just not jump to a conclusion. Let's discuss this with Maya, tomorrow," said Arjun.

"Perfect, rather than eating our minds out, it is better to wait for Maya to answer," concluded Abhimanyu.

Amidst many unanswered queries, Arjun and Abhimanyu forced themselves to calm down and let the night pass. The next day, all the boys woke up early, finished their morning routine and headed to see Maya. On the way to Lakshya, Abhimanyu briefed Rishi and Dhruv about Lakshya going to be demolished.

"Here comes a new problem," said Dhruv.

"We are in more trouble now," said Rishi, sounding concerned.

"Yeah. I know you guys are tensed too, but if Lakshya goes down, we don't know if Maya will still stay there or perish, for which only Maya has the answer," said Arjun, ending to the discussion.

When they reached the gate of the house, the gates opened. The doors of the house slowly opened as the boy's approached the door. The haunted house had no houses nearby, and the road leading to the haunted house was empty and untouched due to the fear of the ghost. They entered the hall and heard the door and the gate close behind them. "MAYA!!!" screamed the boys all at once. Maya magically appeared in front of them.

"Welcome back my heroes," said Maya.

"Hi," said Dhruv.

"I still can't believe I am experiencing this," said Rishi.

"Yes. I couldn't sleep last night because of the anticipation of today," added Abhimanyu. "Ok Maya, we have come here to dig the story even deeper. I haven't been this excited since I finished my semester exam's last week. This excitement that I feel tops the chart of excitement," said Arjun.

"Do you know that Lakshya is going to go down?" enquired Arjun.

"YES!! I knew that destiny would give us a hard time, completing the mission," answered Maya.

"What do you mean???" Arjun questioned.

"Look guys, you all are destined to meet in this life and complete the unfinished mission of our previous birth, so we are bound to meet rivals," clarified Maya.

"Rival... that means Aarav uncle is our rival???" asked Arjun in shock.

"You said we are destined to meet in this life to finish our mission and as we are going to dive into the mission, Aarav uncle comes in, so is he also destined to be in this mission as our rival???" added Rishi before Maya or anyone else could respond.

"You will soon come to know, boys," said Maya.

"So, what's our mission?" We are here to know it in depth,"

Dhruv asked as he looked at Maya. "Yeah," the others said in excitement. "If Lakshya gets demolished, will it affect your soul???" enquired Arjun.

"Yes, Arjun, if Lakshya is destroyed, due to the curse, my soul will not attain eternal bliss and you guys will perish at the age of 22. Now, it is time that you learn in depth about our previous birth and our connection with the ring," said Maya.

Chapter – Three

Digging The Past

"It all began 50 years ago, right here in Kerala." Maya stated.

"All five of us were pursuing Post-graduation in the same college. My name was Laya. Arjun was Sachin. Dhruv was Vamshi. Rishi was known as Vaishnav and Abhimanyu's name was Vikranth. Soon after we started our PG life, our friendship began. Sachin's dad, Sadvik, was a businessman who used to travel abroad. One fine day, while Sadvik was taking a walk on the streets of London, he came across a ring in an antique shop that was so mesmerizing that Sachin's dad could not resist himself buying the ring. He quickly went inside the shop."

"I want that ring," said Sadvik to the shop keeper, pointing at the silver ring with a dark blue stone embarked in the centre.

"Ok," said the shopkeeper. Sadvik paid the price of the ring and left the shop.

On the way home, as soon as Sadvik took the ring out of his pocket and wore it, he was pushed towards the wall of a building by an invisible jolt of power while his eyes were shut. He could visualize in his mind that his dad was making this ring, chanting mantras to make it powerful. He could see that some power being guided inside the ring.

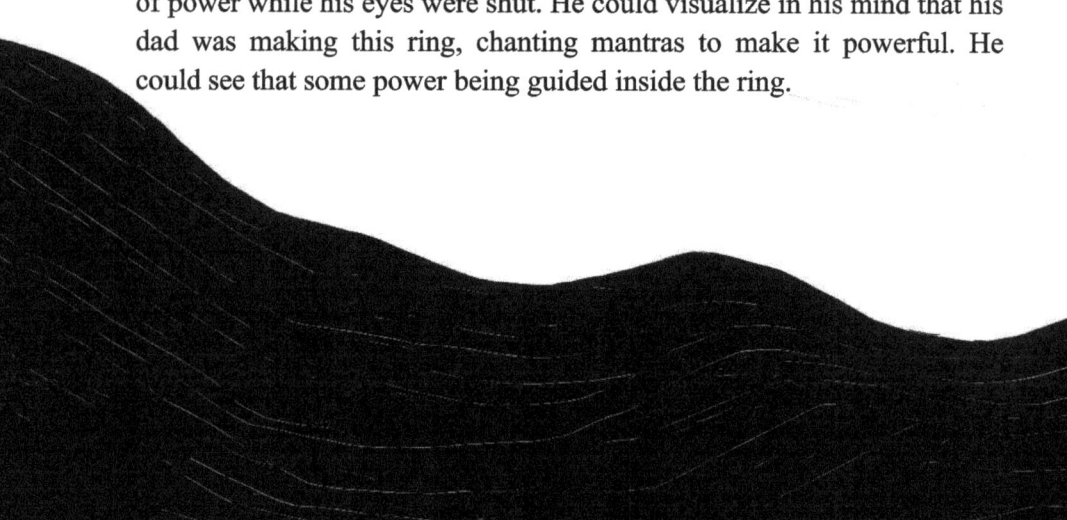

At that exact moment, Sadvik opened his eyes with shock as if he just woke up from a bad dream.

But he felt more confident and powerful than ever. "What was that? Was that a dream? I know that my dad was a black magician, but he never talked about this ring!!! What is this ring doing here in London?" Sadvik murmured.

All these thoughts were running through Sadvik as he reached his hotel in London. Just as he lay down on the brown couch, Sadvik got a call from Manjith, his business partner and closest friend.

"Where were you, Sadvik?" Manjith inquired.

"I just reached my hotel room," replied Sadvik. "Remember, the business deal we planned..." Just as Manjith was about to finish his sentence, Sadvik interrupted. "Yeah. I know, but it hasn't been approved yet, right?" Sadvik asked, sounding disappointed.

"That is why I have been trying to call you. I got it approved. We need to leave for India tomorrow," Manjith replied excitedly. "Really?!!!" Sadvik asked in excitement. "It's true. I got a call from the agency saying that they are interested in building a supermarket by demolishing Lakshya. We need to reach Kerala as soon as possible," confirmed Manjith. "Oh, that is great. But approval took three months?" Sadvik questioned, sounding confused. "Everything happens for good. Anyway, let us pack our bags and leave for India. I shall meet you tomorrow at the port. I have two cruise-ship tickets to Kochi as all flights are booked," told Manjith.

"Ok," said Sadvik, staring at the ring as he hung up the phone.

He could not believe that the business project he planned for so long had finally been approved. He and Manjith had a plan to build a supermarket in Trivandrum, destroying Lakshya. Now, Lakhya is deserted.

Sadvik looked at the ring and said, "Do you have anything to do with the approval? Are you magical? I wanted this approval for so long, and just as I wore you on my finger, I got the approval the very same day." He looked up to the sky and imagined the visuals he saw when he wore the ring for the first time. The next day, Manjith arrived at the port, waiting for Sadvik. "Hey, Manjith, I am here," shouted Sadvik, waving his hand.

"Oh, just in time," said Manjith.

"Yeah. Our ship will leave for India in half an hour. Let us just wait in the queue," said Sadvik, pointing toward the queue in line to board the ship.

"Wow! Where did you get this??" Manjith questioned, looking at the ring as they reached the queue.

"It is beautiful, isn't it? I got it yesterday from an antique shop," clarified Sadvik.

"You know what???" Sadvik said, looking at the ring.

"What?? Manjith asked as they slowly approached the ship entrance.

"I think this ring is........" Suddenly, Sadvik stopped as it was his turn to show the ticket to the guard of the ship. Sadvik and Manjith showed their tickets and made themselves comfortable.

"You were about to say something, right??? Manjith asked Sadvik.

"Oh, that..." said Sadvik as he carefully placed his bag.

"Give me your bag," said Sadvik, gesturing at Manjith's bag. "Here it is," said Manjith and gave Sadvik his black bag. Sadvik kept his bag next to his red bag.

"We only have two bags to carry," said Sadvik.

"Yeah, as you know all other luggage will reach Kochi port in a cargo ship by the time we reach there," said Manjith.

"That is good," said Sadvik in content. Manjith noticed Sadvik was silent on the journey and was always staring at the ring.

"Hey, Sadvik, why are you always staring at the ring?" Manjith questioned.

Sadvik looked at Manjith as if he was in shock to see Manjith sitting opposite to him because Sadvik was lost in thought always looking at the new ring.

"What is the deal with the ring?" Manjith asked, losing his patience.

"Let's go to the deck where there are only a few people," whispered Sadvik.

"Ok," said Manjith. Sadvik and Manjith walked toward the deck.

They stopped at a corner of the deck. Sadvik was in dual minds whether to share the experience he felt while he wore the ring or to keep it a secret. But, in a deep breath, he narrated the visual he saw when he wore the ring and also told Manjith whether the approval was a magic of the ring. As soon as Sadvik finished the narration, Manjith burst into laughter. Passengers were less on the deck, but the people who were on the deck stared at Manjith.

"Can you bring your voice down??" A passenger questioned in anger.

"I am sorry," replied Manjith, tilting his head to everyone at the deck, clearly embarrassed. "Look, Manjith, I know you don't believe my experience. But I am not lying," demanded Sadvik.

"Let me get this straight. When you wore the ring, the experience you felt might have been because your subconscious mind remembered your dad and his black magic; that is the reason you had this imagination. Don't tell anyone about this. They will laugh at you the way I laughed," said Manjith.

"But, right when I wore the ring, why did I visualize that? I knew my dad was a black magician since I was a child, I could have had that visual long back???"

Sadvik questioned in confusion. "No one can answer that buddy what you experienced is in your mind. The approval on the very day you wore the ring can just a coincidence," stated Manjith.

"That could be a coincidence. But what about the visuals I saw when I wore the ring," Sadvik asked Manjith.

"All I can say is that you forget about the magic in the ring, and just consider the ring as an ordinary fashion ring," said Manjith.

"Yeah, I am trying, but the visual keeps emerging in my mind," said Sadvik.

"If you are so much into the ring, when we reach Kochi, you go, see any black magician and get to the bottom of it," said Manjith.

"Thanks, that is a great idea," said Sadvik in relief.

"While that is out of the way, shall we have a cup of tea?" Manjith asked as he wanted Sadvik to have these thoughts off the ring.

"Definitely," answered Sadvik, as they walked towards the tea stall on the deck.

Sadvik and Manjith went back to their seats talking about issues that interested both. Days passed, and the ship reached its destination safely. Sadvik and Manjith walked towards the exit of the port.

"Over here," shouted Sachin from outside the gate, waving to Sadvik and Manjith.

Sadvik and Manjith walked towards Sachin. Sachin hugged Sadvik in excitement. Laya was happy to see her dad Manjith, as she ran to hug him. Sadvik shook Laya's hand and Manjith shook Sachin's hand as a gesture to greet each other.

"Good evening, dad; good evening, uncle." Sachin greeted them.

"Very good evening, son," said Sadvik and Manjith in chorus. "Where is our car?" Sadvik enquired. "It is right there," said Sachin, pointing to a black Ambassador parked in the parking lot. Sachin helped with their luggage that came in a cargo ship. Sachin sat in the driver's seat; Laya sat next to him in the passenger seat. Sadvik and Manjith sat in the back seat.

"How was your trip?" Sachin enquired.

"It was good until we got the approval call; after the approval call, we just wanted to come back," said Sadvik, smiling.

Watching Sachin and Laya, Sadvik just patted Manjith and gestured as if to say, 'They look fabulous when they are together.' Manjith gave a gesture that suggested, 'I know.'

"Dad, when will they demolish Lakshya??" Laya asked.

"Probably in a week," answered Manjith.

Sadvik and Manjith went to their respective houses, which were close to each other. While Sadvik and Sachin were having dinner, Sachin noticed the ring in his dad's finger.

"Wow, dad, that is a nice ring. You bought it from London???" Sachin enquired.

"Yeah, this ring was very captivating, so I bought it and..." Suddenly, Sadhvik stopped; he was about to tell the experience he felt when he put the ring but decided against it, thinking of Manjith's reaction to the story.

"And what, dad???" Sachin asked.

"Sachin, how are you two doing?" Sadvik asked, hinting at Sachin and Laya's relationship. "Good," said Sachin, feeling quite proud.

"Once both of you finish your studies and find a job, we will take your relationship to the next level. I have already talked to Manjith; he is also fine with this decision," confirmed Sadvik.

"Thank you, dad," said Sachin, who could not control his excitement and hugged Sadvik.

Sadvik looked stunned but smiled as Sachin walked off. On the way to the building to collect the approval paper, Sadvik and Manjith got out of the car and walked towards the building when two random strangers tried to snatch the briefcase that Sadvik was holding, thinking that it had money. Manjith was kicked on his chest and fell on the ground. This agitated Sadvik, who ran behind the two thieves and caught them, threw the suitcase towards Manjith, who was thirty feet away. Sadvik punched the miscreants so hard on their stomachs that blood started to ooze from their mouths. Watching this, onlookers came in and trashed those two goons and called the police. By this time, Manjith was watching in horror and shock.

Sadvik ran towards him, now sitting Manjith and asked, "Are you ok??" asked Sadvik, who picked up the suitcase which lay next to Manjith.

"Now, I am okay," replied Manjith.

"What got into you?" Manjith asked in shock how Sadvik had thrashed the goons.

"I don't know; normally, I am not this powerful," said Sadvik, looking at the ring.

"Your punch was lethal, to say the least," added Manjith.

Now, Manjith was also staring at Sadvik's ring. He thought, 'This is the same ring my dad was searching for. I have never seen him this strong. He didn't even break a sweat. He isn't even tired after all of this commotion. He threw the suitcase thirty feet far and that too after running behind them. It is impossible for any human. This ring is magical as Sadvik had mention. I want the ring.'

"I NEED IT," shouted Manjtth out loud in anger.

"What do you need???" Sadvik enquired as to Manjith's sudden outburst. Manjith was in shock. He was short of words, and with a stutter, he said, "Approval."

"Are you fine???" Sadvik asked, watching Manjith in a pool of sweat.

"Yeah, totally," replied Manjith, wiping his sweat with a handkerchief.

"Then let's head to the building," said Sadvik.

"Ok, let us hurry up," said Manjith as his thoughts were still on the ring.

After Sadvik and Manjith got done with the date of demolition, they walked towards the car. That evening, Manjith instigated Sadvik that they go visit Lakshya that night. Sadvik and Manjith walked into the gate, and Sadvik noticed three people were already inside the compound.

"Who are you???" Sadvik asked in anger.

Manjith just walked back and closed the gates, looked at the surroundings as to be sure that no one was passing by.

"Why did you close the gate???" Sadvik asked Manjith.

"I have some unfinished business with you," Manjith replied. The other three men were surrounding Sadvik. "What business??" Sadvik asked, visibly confused. "That is, you have..." said a guy, Sadvik turned towards the guy, seizing the opportunity. Manjith, who was behind Sadvik, pulled out a knife and stabbed Sadvik from the back. Sadvik turned towards Manjith in pain. Sadvik couldn't believe his childhood friend had betrayed him, and he fell on the ground.

"Don't give me that look. I am the king of betrayal. That was easier than I thought. If pinning you down was this easy, I would not have brought in these people. Ha ha ha. You know what! My dad wanted the ring so badly that day; he drugged your dad while they were having a drink. My dad later made it look like a car accident due to drug overdose, but all of it went in vain because your dad was wearing a replica of the real ring that night when my dad killed your dad. Later, my dad found out that the original ring was stolen. My dad searched everywhere for the ring, but he couldn't find it," said Manjith, proudly laughing. "Now, on to my business," said Manjith as he leaned down and lifted Sadvik's right hand and looked at his fingers. Manjith was in shock. "Where is your ring??" Manjith shouted in anger as he pulled Sadvik by his collar.

Sadvik could not speak because of the pain. When Manjith was about to continue his questioning, he heard a car coming in.

"Guys, quick, pick him up and take him to that hospital where my friend is working, I want that ring. I want him alive until I get that ring," said Manjith to his three men. Sadvik was picked up by Manjith's men and put in their car. His men drove away and admitted Sadvik who was unconscious to the hospital. While Manjith walked towards his house gate, he noticed Laya talking to Sachin.

Sachin ran to him and asked, "Uncle, do you know where my dad is??"

Manjith was taken by surprise by the timing of the question.

"He... he might have gone out for some business activity," said Manjith stuttering. "Oh my god, how did he go without intimating? When I came back from college, he wasn't at home," said Sachin, sounding disturbed.

"You came from college, now?" Manjith enquired.

"Yes, uncle, I was with my friends Vamshi, Vaishnav and Vikrant in the library," said Sachin. "What was Laya up to??? Normally, you guys hang out together. You are like five fingers," Manjith asked.

"Dad, I was there at the library until 5, then I came back home," clarified Laya.

"Ok. Ok Sachin, you better get back home," said Manjith in an attempt to avoid Sachin. "Right uncle, I shall go home. It is already late."

"Bye, Laya," said Sachin as he waved to Laya.

"Bye, Sachin," said Laya as she followed Manjith back home.

Manjith was lost in thought that night about the ring.

'Where is the ring? I will have to dig the ring location from Sadvik by hook or by crook.' Manjith murmured. He heard a knock on his door.

"Dad, can I come in??" Laya asked from outside the door.

"Door is open," replied Manjith, sitting from the bed. She walked in and sat next to Manjith.

"Dad, do you believe in supernatural power?" enquired Laya.

"It may exist; I would say it may be a reality. Why do you ask?" Manjith said completely baffled as to the question and its timing.

"Sachin told me that Sadvik uncle has a ring that is supernatural.". Laya said.

"Oh!!! A Supernatural ring??? Why didn't Sadvik tell me about it?" Sadvik replied.

"Oh. Sachin has the ring now. He said he will go to Lakshya tonight and bury it there," said Laya.

"WHAT?? Why would he do that???" Manjith asked in shock.

'I need to get to Lakshya before he gets there,' thought Manjith.

"I don't know, dad. Sadvik uncle told Sachin to wear the ring for one last time and bury it before people find out the power in it. Sachin obeyed his dad. He has some belief in supernatural power in the ring," said Laya.

Manjith ran towards the main door, "Laya close the door, I forgot some important stuff to do," said Manjith as he vanished into the night. Laya was taken aback by her dad's sudden reaction. Manjith ran to Lakshya as fast as his legs could take him. He saw his men coming towards his house. He got into the car and asked, "Did you talk to the doctor?"

"Yes, boss. The doctor said since you helped the doctor in a time of crisis earlier, he shall not call the cops since he recognized the stab wound and shall call you once Sadvik gains consciousness," replied a goon.

"If you guys cheat me and try to take the ring, I shall kill each and everyone in your family." Manjith threatened his men. His men were visibly scared; they nodded in agreement. Manjith reached Lakhya and noticed no one was there. He hid in a corner with his men and waited there, he heard bikes approaching the gate. It was Sachin, Vamshi, Vikrant and Vaishnav. They opened the gate and closed it.

"Go Sachin," Said Vamshi. Sachin wore the ring and he did not have any experience what his dad had told. Vikrant and Vaishnav walked with Sachin towards the main door.

"Dig it there!!!" said Vamshi, pointing to a corner.

"Yeah, this seems to be the right spot," said Sachin.

"Now, look Sachin, it is your dad's ring and only you have the right to know the digging place. We will turn our backs, and you go dig it anywhere you want," said Vikrant.

"But we are in this together," clarified Sachin.

"He is right. We are in this together, but you have the right to do it. Now, go," said Vamshi as he walked towards Vikrant.

"There is your heartthrob, Laya, now go," said Vaishnav.

Sachin came close to Laya and asked, "What took you so long?"

"My dad was at home," replied Laya.

"We need to keep this to ourselves," said Sachin.

Laya was embarrassed on herself that she disclosed the secret information to her dad. "Hey Romeo, just finish what we came for," said Vamshi looking at Sachin.

"GO!!" said Laya.

Sachin ran towards the back of Lakshya. Manjith didn't know that her daughter was in this too, as he was hiding at the back. As he saw Sachin running towards the back, Manjith turned to his men and said, "Kill everyone; make sure no one goes out of here alive." Manjith climbed out of the house, not noticing his daughter was running behind Sachin. Laya and the others noticed three men opening the gate of Lakshya. All three men ran behind the youngsters. "Sachin... we have company," said Vikrant shouting.

Sachin didn't have time to remove the ring... he ran as fast as he could. It was chaos. Vikrant was being hit on the head by one of the goons when Vamshi stepped in to save Vikrant; he got stabbed, too. "Two down and three to go," said a goon.

Laya was hiding in a corner as Sachin ran and hid next to her. They heard the screams of Vikrant and Vamshi.

Sachin said, "You stay here," and ran towards them and kicked one of the goons to the ground. Laya was crying. One of the goons grabbed Laya and cut her throat.

Sachin was the only one left. Viashnav was already dead. Sachin's anger was at the max as he punched and kicked all three goons, but they kept stabbing him. Finally, all three men surrounded Sachin and killed him. One of the goons went out and searched for Manjith. Manjith came running from a corner as he saw one of his men calling his name.

"Take all the bodies and bikes away. There should be no proof," ordered Manjith as he took the ring from Sachin's dead body.

"Yes, boss," said three men as they were dragging all bodies and pushing the bike away. Manjith was so thrilled and laughed in pride. But he remembered what Sadvik had said to him when he wore the ring for the first time. Manjith didn't experience that feeling; he knew that the ring was useless as he tried to lift the bike, which should be an easy task with the power of the ring, but he could not lift the bike. All his efforts and killing were of no use.

He thought, 'Why is the ring not powerful?' He screamed in despair. He felt a pain in his chest as he screamed. Manjith noticed one of the goons bringing a young girl's dead body. Manjith ran towards her body and was in shock. He could not believe that he ordered to kill his own daughter. In anger, he shot all the goons. Manjith was crying and fell on the ground to breathe his last breath. He was a heart patient who had two attacks before.

Later that night, Sadvik also passed away at the hospital. Since many murders happened in Lakshya, it was termed Haunted House from then. The proposal to bring Lakshya down was never to be heard again. Back to reality, Maya finished her story as all the boys were eagerly sitting there as if listening to a movie story.

Chapter – Four

Mission Here We Come

Maya looked at the boys who were staring at her as if to say 'Continue with the story.'

"BOYS!" Maya said. They looked at Maya like they were in the middle of a movie and Maya disturbed them, "That is the end of the story."

Maya confirmed. "Oh..." said the boys in a dejected voice.

"Our mission is to find the ring??" Arjun asked. "Or stop Lakshya from coming down?" Abhimanyu interrupted.

"Both. Lakshya should not come down, and the ring should be found," said Maya.

"Where do we start??" Rishi asked.

"We don't know the exact location of the ring, but it is here in Lakshya. When Sadvik died, the ring disappeared and since the ring was created here in Lakshay. Sachin had the ring when he died; the ring is here somewhere." Maya added.

"Since you know this much of the story, how come you don't know where the ring is?" Dhruv asked in confusion.

"Because I was the reason of our death last birth, I can't get to know where the ring is. Only Arjun can unleash the ring's true power, because he had the ring at the time of his death, and he is the rightful owner of the ring this birth too," answered Maya looking at Arjun.

"Then why didn't your dad get cursed. He is the one who masterminded our killing?" Abhimanyu asked.

"The ring has a curse. Whoever discloses the ring bearer to a person and if that person kills the ring bearer, the one who disclosed the information will roam as a soul till the ring is brought back to its rightful owner," clarified Maya.

"So that means if Arjun finds the ring, and we stop Lakshya from destruction, our mission is done??" Abhimanyu questioned Maya.

"It is not as simple as it sounds. After my dad died, the ring disappeared and is hidden in Lakshya. Aarav is the re-incarnation of my dad and Vishnu is the re-incarnation of Sadvik," said Maya.

Before Maya could continue, Arjun said, "What? My dad is also an incarnation? Does dad know all about this???"

Maya replied, "Your dad could be totally unaware of the ring. It is best that you don't ask him about this since if he is unaware about the past life. You may have a hard time in convincing him about the ring and the backstory because not everyone believes in rebirth and a powerful ring."

"Yes, let's not drag dad into this danger," said Abhimanyu.

"You are right," Arjun said.

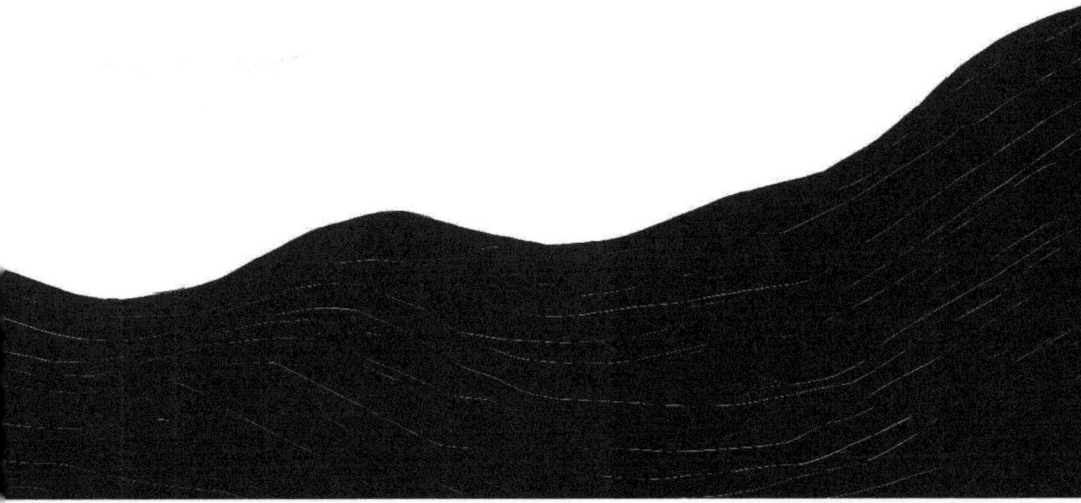

Dhruv said, "So, Aarav uncle is Arjun's rival in this life."

"Unfortunately, it is true. Aarav might be bringing this down to find the ring," Maya replied.

"Why is Lakshya so important?" Arjun asked.

"Lashya is actually a sacred place where Sadvik's dad did black magic rituals to make the ring powerful. Since Arjun is related to Lakshya by his previous birth, he has the duty to protect Lakshya; the ring bearer has to protect Lakshya because, in his last birth, he was unable to protect Lakshya and the ring," said Maya.

"The biggest problem is that we don't know where we start searching from and how long the search will take place," said Rishi concerned.

"Sadvik's dad was a power seeker who put his heart into Lakshya. Since he wanted power, he created the ring and made a clause that the ring bearer had to protect Lakshya or he would die. His curse also mentioned that whoever tries to save the ring should save it, or else they will die, and so Sachin's friends died. It is that curse that says if the ring bearer and his friends don't protect the ring and Lakshya, even their reincarnation will die at the same age as the previous birth until Lakshya and the ring are in deserving hands. So as Sadvik's friends in the previous birth and Arjun's brother and friends in this birth, it is all your responsibility to find the ring and protect Lakshya," said Maya.

Arjun said, "We are in this together; we have this unfinished task to do. Our lives have a purpose. The ring will be found, and Lakshya will be protected, right guys???" sounding determined and confident.

"OH, YES," Shouted the boys.

"But what kind of a curse is that? If you don't do this and that, you die now and next time too???" Dhruv questioned in anger.

"Curses are a part of our history, Dhruv; even Lord Krishna was cursed," added Maya.

"This is unbelievable; I can't contain my shock in knowing that you all were my friends in my last birth," said Rishi, quite emotionally.

"Everything is destiny. Last month, we treated Lakshya as a mere haunted house, and now, our life depends on it," said Abhimanyu.

"We still don't know how Sadvik's dad lost the ring," asked Arjun.

"Sadvik's dad created the ring, but it was stolen when he was on a trip to London. The thief saw the ring, thought it was precious, stole it and sold it to that antique shop from where Sadvik bought it," answered Maya.

"Sadvik's dad, Sadvik, and now Arjun, that means the ring can be controlled only by Sadvik's dad's lineage??" Rishi enquired.

"And Why couldn't Manjith uncle control the ring?" Arjun added this doubt to Maya.

"Sadvik was the actual ring controller; even though he gave the ring to Sachin, Sachin couldn't control it because Sadvik was still alive when Sachin wore the ring. If the actual ring owner is alive, the ring can't be controlled by anyone else. When Sachin died, Manjith stole the ring from Sachin, and hence, Manjith didn't get the power of the ring as anyone else other than the actual ring bearer couldn't have the power of the ring. Now, Arjun is the ring master, so if he gives it to Rishi or anyone else, the ring won't show its power. Arjun's next generation can only enjoy the ring's power after him," clarified Maya

"So, can I own the power of the ring??" asked Abhimanyu.

"No, the rightful owner is Arjun; only he can enjoy the ring's power. Even if Arjun is killed for the ring, the ring will vanish the moment his soul leaves his body." Maya answered Abhimanyu.

"That means that the ring is just a fashion item for everybody else except Arjun," Rishi said "Yes," stated Maya. "Then what is the problem??" asked Dhruv.

"Hey, Dhruv, if you want to ask a question, ask it completely; we are not mind readers," said Rishi.

"What I meant was, if the ring is useless for others, why do people try to steal it?" stated Dhruv.

"The people stealing the ring don't know that the ring is useless for them, like Manjith uncle, who saw Sadvik uncle's unnatural strength and killed him for the ring. If anyone else sees the ring bearer with unnatural power, they might end up fatally injuring that person or vice versa for the ring." Arjun said.

"And that is the reason Arjun needs to keep the ring with him safely as he is the rightful owner of the ring," said Abhimanyu.

"That is right," said Maya.

"This place..." Said Arjun, tilting his head around the roof of Lakshya, "...is where we met our end the last time for the ring, and now, we are here together again for the ring." The boys looked at Arjun in a paranoid expression. None of them could believe that they all were together in their last birth and died together.

"When will the demolition begin??" Rishi enquired.

"Next week, I guess. Aarav uncle will be coming for demolition next week," answered Arjun.

"Will he be aware of our relationship from our previous births?" Dhruv asked, sounding concerned. "He might be aware; we don't know," said Maya.

"But he may be bringing Lakshya just for his shopping mall," said Abhimanyu.

"Anyway, boys, we need to start fast. We need to find the ring and stop the demolition as soon as possible," said Maya, sounding concerned.

"Maya, what if the ring bearer with the power of the ring does bad deeds?"

Dhruv enquired Arjun's eyes were looked onto Maya. Maya looked back at Arjun and said, "You can't; the ring will only assist the ring bearer in good deeds."

Arjun had a sigh of relief, knowing that even with great power, he would not go into the path of evil.

"You guys better leave; we will meet soon. The ring might be buried anywhere in Lakshya," added Maya.

"So, we need to dig this half-acre plot for the ring, how deep do we dig. We are not sure where the ring is buried here?" A surprised Abhimanyu asked.

"We might as well have to risk it, our fate is at stake," said Maya.

'Wow! This just keeps on getting better and better," said Rishi in sarcasm.

"It is impossible to dig this huge area in the morning; people will notice the digging, and it will be all downhill from there. We can't dig at night since it will be dark, and we won't be able to search the area we dug properly," said Arjun.

"Yeah, if my dad comes to know that I dig here, my appointment with our family doctor is confirmed," said Dhruv visibly tensed.

"Wait, we don't have to dig this whole area. You need to find a metal detector from somewhere and scan the area and dig in the area where the metal detector beeps. We need to find a way to do the digging without any-one noticing," said Maya.

"Where do we get a metal detector?" Rishi enquired. Arjun was busy remembering something when he heard the word metal detector, "Oh, yes, my colleague from College who is very close to Shalini said that her dad had a metal detector. We might be able to obtain one from her," said Arjun.

"Perfect, this is a start to the mission. Tomorrow, try to get the metal detector from her and let's try to find the ring," said Maya, sounding happy.

"So, tomorrow is the official start of our mission," said Arjun.

"Yeah," said Maya. "We need to stop the demolition also." Dhruv added to the worry. The boys turned to Maya in anticipation. "We can't stop the demolition beforehand because the neighborhood is happy that Lakshya, the 'haunted house' is going down. If you guys just say the demolition should be stopped, you don't have a reason to say why??? People will not believe in our story. We need to wait till the demolition day to stop the demolition somehow," clarified Maya.

"And how do we stop the demolition that day?" Rishi enquired.

"Destiny will show us a way. For now, you guys leave. We will meet tomorrow as planned; you need to find a metal detector, and we will start our mission," said Maya with confidence.

"With the metal detector, we can do the scanning tomorrow evening, because Uncle Madhav's daugher's wedding party is tomorrow at 6PM. Our layout will be empty tomorrow as the party hall is 40km away and three buses are booked for us to go. The only thing is we all need to find a reason to skip the party. We only need to dig the area where the metal detector beeps," said Arjun.

"Brilliant, as for the scanning, you all don't need to be here. Any two will do, especially Arjun should be here," said Maya.

"No, we are in this together," said Rishi

"Yeah," said Abhimanyu and Dhruv.

"Ok then, please find a way to skip the party tomorrow, so you all can be here in the evening," said Maya.

The boys looked determined to complete the mission, as they waved their magical friend bye and headed out. Arjun walked with the boys who were busy chit-chatting about how powerful Arjun would be when he found the ring.

"Arjun will be our Superman," said Rishi.

"He is my brother, and that is why he was blessed to be the ring bearer," said Abhimanyu in pride.

"Oh please, his fear will be that you are in this as well," replied Dhruv.

Abhimanyu noticed that Arjun was not paying attention to them because Arjun would not counter Abhimanyu's sentence.

"Arjun," called Abhimanyu, patting Arjun with his hands.

The others turned to Arjun. Arjun was jolted as if he had been woken up from his sleep by Abhimanyu.

"What are you thinking?" Abhimanyu asked.

"I... was thinking about all these things revolving around us," stated Arjun.

"Yeah, even we can't believe it," said Abhimanyu.

"It is a do-or-die mission for us," said a concerned Arjun.

The boys were suddenly motionless after Arjun's statement.

"We need to accept the reality and complete the mission." Arjun said.

"Yeah, we got to do what we have to do," said Dhruv Just when Rishi was about to say something. He noticed his dad walking and said, "My dad is coming this way," Others looked straight at the road and saw Rishi's dad.

"Guys, so here is the plan. This evening, let us try to get the metal detector from Shalini. We will meet at the road connecting to her house at 4 PM today. We will decide how we all will skip the party tomorrow evening," whispered Arjun.

Other boys nodded as they walked towards their layout.

"Hello uncle," greeted Arjun. "Hello Arjun," replied Rishi's dad. "Where are you going, dad??" Rishi asked in curiosity. "Out for a walk," Rishi's dad replied. "Where were you guys??" Rishi's dad questioned as he looked at Rishi.

Rishi suddenly remembered that he had told his dad they were going to play cricket when he ran out of the house that morning and came to know that none of them had a bat or ball in their hand.

"Walking dad, we thought of playing cricket, but we didn't get the ball we lost two days back," said Rishi before anyone could reply. "Ok. Then why don't you guys buy a new ball," said Rishi's dad as he took money from his pocket and handed it to Rishi.

"Thanks dad. But we all have put money and have enough to buy a ball. Isn't it right guys???" Rishi said, giving a look to Dhruv and Abhimanyu that it is high time they stepped in to agree with the cooked-up story.

"Yes uncle, we will buy the ball in the evening," said Abhimanyu. "In the evening, we shall go for a walk and buy the ball to play."

"Now, the shop is closed," Dhruv intervened. Rishi gave them both a look that suggested, 'Well played, guys'. "Fine," said Rishi's dad as he walked past them. "DAD," Rishi Shouted, and his dad suddenly stopped. "Here, take this." Rishi handed the money back to his dad. Rishi's dad smiled at Rishi proudly; he kept the money back in his pocket and walked off. The boys walked to their houses in anticipation of what lies ahead. The clock ticked 3:30 PM.

Abhimanyu and Arjun were outside their gate when noticed Rishi and Dhruv walking toward them. They continued their walk towards Shalini's house. "What is our plan?" Enquired Dhruv. "Wait and watch," said Abhimanyu. "What do you mean wait and watch???"

Asked a shocked Rishi. "Yeah," said Dhruv in shock. "I called Shalini a while back and said that I need a metal detector for an experiment," said Arjun. "What did she say?" Rishi asked. "She said her dad should give a green signal for that," replied Abhimanyu. "So, we ask her dad," said Dhruv looking tensed. "If we all go, he might doubt us. So, you guys stay away from her house. I will go and talk to uncle," said Arjun. The boys nodded in approval. They reached the road where they could see Shalini's house. Arjun reached the gate.

The boys hiding behind a tree thumbed Arjun good luck. Arjun breathed a sigh of confidence and opened the gate. Arjun noticed Shalini coming out of the main door. Her house was big with cream and light yellow paint. He noticed that there was a store room on the right to him with an old metal detector lying inside.

The main door was 40 feet from the gate, and a garden with beautiful flowers on the left side mesmerized Arjun. As Shalini was waving Arjun, her dog Buddy ran towards Arjun and started licking him. "Buddy," Shalini shouted. Buddy pretended not to hear her command. Shalini ran towards Arjun and caught Buddy's collar.

"It's ok. Let him do what he wants to do," Arjun said. "He still remembers you," Said Shalini as she let Buddy free. Buddy just ran all over the compound to show his excitement. "Yeah. We both got our puppies on the same day from the same place" said Arjun.

"Buddy and Ricky are best friends just like us" Shalini added. Arjun was taken aback by "best friend" remark "Absolutely, where is uncle?" Arjun changed the topic, "Oh, Sorry. I completely forgot. Dad is inside. Come on in," said Shalini. Arjun smiled and walked with Shalini towards the main door.

Once they reached inside, Arjun noticed a healthy Army retired officer sitting on a white couch in the spacious hall. "Oh, Arjun. Sit," said Kalidas, Shalini's dad. Arjun sat on the couch. Shalini sat next to him, and Buddy sat in front of them on the floor. "So. How are you, son??" questioned Kalidas. "I am fine, uncle. How are you?" asked Arjun. "I am fine, Arjun; post retirement life is peaceful. That reminds me, Shalini told me that you needed a metal detector for some experiment??" asked Kalidas. Arjun looked at Kalidas and replied, "Yes uncle, I need a metal detector just for 2-3 days. I have holidays now, and I thought, why not put my time to good use. I found some science experiment videos on YouTube and want to try it out myself."

"That is wonderful that kids of your age want to do something creative other than staring at the phone screen 24/7. There is a metal detector in the store room, I get it for you," said Kalidas as he went through the steps to his room. Arjun was thrilled that Kalidas had bought his story. "How is your family, Arjun?" asked Shalini, patting Buddy. "They are fine. How is aunty?" replied Arjun. "She is doing fine. She is in Melbourne for a business trip," said Shalini. "Oh, that is great," acknowledged Arjun. Kalidas walked down the stairs with a black colour metal detector in hand. Arjun stood up in excitement, 'Here, Arjun, this is what you are looking for; the power button is here, and when you take this near a metal object, it will beep," said Kalidas as he demonstrated it.

Arjun had the metal detector in hand. Buddy suddenly woke up, scanned the metal detector and gave his approval. "Thanks, uncle and Shalini." Arjun said. "Cut the formality; care for a cup of tea?" Shalini asked. "No, thank you. I am in a hurry. I have to go to my friend's house. Bye,

Uncle," said Arjun. "Bye." Kalidas replied. "Bye, Shalini," Arjun said, rubbing Buddy. "Bye, buddy," said Arjun. "Bye, Arjun." Shalini replied. Arjun stormed outside the gate, closed it and kept the metal detector tucked behind his shirt. He walked towards the tree where the boys were patiently waiting. "Here, he comes." Abhimanyu said. Rishi and Dhruv looked at Arjun with waited breath.

Abhimanyu saw that Arjun had nothing in his hand but was taking on his phone. "Bajarangbali. I think he didn't get the detector. His hand is empty,' said Abhimanyu, tensed. Dhruv and Rishi were about to express their feeling when Arjun, after making sure that no one was noticing, pulled the metal detector out of his shirt.

Abhimanyu hugged Arjun in excitement; Rishi and Dhruv screamed in thrill. "Quiet. People will notice us," said Arjun while he put his phone back in his pocket after finishing the call. "This is great," said Abhimanyu. "You did it," said Dhruv. "The mission is on," Rishi said. "Listen, guys. I will keep this with me. If my dad or mom asks, I will tell them that I took it for an experiment. As of tomorrow, to skip the function, I had said to my dad this afternoon that I need to visit my friend at the hospital."

"Abhi is coming with me too. I told him that it was our friend, Preetham who used to play with us before he shifted his house. So, I told my dad to ask Rishi's and Dhruv's parents to send you guys with us," said Arjun. 'Just now, as I was exiting Shalini's house, my dad called me and said Rishi and Dhruv will come with me and Abhi tomorrow evening, as both of your parents agreed." Arjun explained. Rishi and Dhruv jumped up in excitement.

Abhimanyu looked at Arjun in a look as if to say, 'You are so brilliant and handle things in your own way with intelligence'. Arjun and the boys walked back to their homes, filled with excitement and joy. They headed their way home. Arjun, since waking up, was thrilled about what was in store that day.

Abhimanyu was already up and watching TV. Vishnu was about to take Ricky out for a walk. Anjali was busy preparing breakfast. Arjun washed his face, brushed his teeth and stood near the pooja room next to the stairs leading to the bedroom. "Anjali. I am off for a walk with Ricky," said Vishnu "Ok. By the time you are back, breakfast will be ready," added Anjali. "Great, remember we will go out at 11:00 am to buy a gift with some neighbours," said Vishnu. Arjun and Abhimanyu looked at each other and smiled. "Oh, Arjun, you are awake," Vishnu asked. "Yeah, dad," replied Arjun. Anjali came from the kitchen and handed Arjun a cup of tea. "Thanks, mom," said Arjun. "You are welcome," replied Anjali with a smile. That evening, Vishnu got a call from their neighbour that it was time to head to the reception.

Vishnu peeped through the window and saw Arjun, Abhimaanyu, Dhruv and Rishi standing outside their gate, and a bus was standing next to the boys. "Anjali," Vishnu shouted. "Coming," replied Anjali. Anjali came down from the stairs in a designer saree. Vishnu wore a Black jacket with a white shirt and brown pants. "Let's go." Vishnu said. Arjun came in and said, "Dad, I will have the main door key," as Arjun took the main key from the key bunch.

Vishnu heard a horn and saw that the bus was getting full and that another bus was coming from behind. "Ok. So, let us leave, Arjun. Be careful, and drive the car with caution. On the way, fill with diesel. How is your friend now?" Anjali enquired with concern. "He is still not out of the woods," said Arjun. "Everything will be fine. You stay safe. Take care, kids." Vishnu said, and Anjali followed Vishnu; they got into the bus and waved to Abhimanyu and Arjun bye.

Dhruv's parents got into the bus and sat behind Vishnu and Anjali. The bus started; the boys waved bye until the bus disappeared from their sight. Arjun ran to his room, took the metal detector, ran towards the main door and locked it. He called Ricky and closed the gate. The boys noticed that all the houses in the street leading to Lakshya were empty.

They reached Lakshya. Arjun opened the gates and made his way inside; the boys were right behind him along with Ricky. Arjun opened the main door and called on Maya. The spirit came in front of him. "We got the metal detector," Arjun said in excitement. Maya looked at the boys in admiration. "So, we need to scan the compound first. Arjun, you scan the compound; Abimanyu will assist you."

"Rishi and Dhruv will scan once you guys finish". Arjun and Abhimanyu searched for the ring, taking hours, but they could not find it. Arjun and

Rishi checked inside Lakshya inch-by-inch, too, but in vain. Maya was frustrated like the boys. "Where is the ring???" Arjun asked. "This means only one thing; the ring might come to you only in your hardest time," added Maya in despair. "So that means if Arjun doesn't go through a do-or-die situation to stop their demolition, the ring won't come to him," Dhruv asked. "Unfortunately, it is true." Maya added.

"The ring will come to you; don't worry. Now, our concentration should be to stop the demolition," Maya said. "Yeah, if I have to go through hardest time to get the ring, I will accept that I am in for a storm," said Arjun. Abhimanyu was not at all happy with the do-or-die situation that Arjun would have to go through if the ring had to come to him.

"Whatever it is, we are with you," said Abhimanyu. "Yes, we are in this together," said Rishi and Dhruv. "Thanks, guys, we better move," said Arjun. Maya nodded in approval. They left Lakshya and went home. Ricky followed them with a stick he found from Lakshya. After 2-3 days, Arjun was busy on his phone when he got a call from Shalini. "Good morning, Arjun," Shalini said. "Good morning, Shalini," replied Arjun. "I have a request for you." Shalini stopped "Shoot." Arjun replied. "We will be out of town; we are going to my cousin's house. So, can you please feed Buddy while we are gone???" Asked Shalini. "Don't worry. I will feed Buddy until you come back. Anyway, our college doesn't open until next month, so I will be at home," said Arjun. "Thank you." Shalini said.

"How are you travelling?" asked Arjun. "By flight," clarified Shalini. "Ok," Arjun said. "I have kept food for Buddy. I will give it to you in the afternoon. "Shalini said. "We feed Ricky the same food you feed Buddy; you didn't have to buy food for Buddy for one week." Arjun was interrupted by Shalini. "It is ok, Arjun. Since I bought food, it will stay in the fridge; it is better you give that food to Buddy," said Shalini "Oh, Planning," Laughed Arjun. "I am your friend. So, I need to keep up with you, right," said Shalini. Arjun laughed the last comment off. Arjun wished Shalini, "Happy journey, have fun," and they finished their chit-chat.

Chapter – Five

The Final Showdown

The do-or-die day finally arrived. The boys who were already at Lakshya gates witnessed Vivaan and Aarav, giving orders to construction workers on how to proceed with the demolition. Arjun, like the other boys, had fear on his face when he stood behind the gates, thinking, 'If I fail to find the ring and protect Lakshya from falling, it is the end of our lives. The Do-or-Die situation is here. We don't have a definite plan to complete our mission.'

"What is our plan?" Abhimanyu asked, staring at Arjun.

Arjun scanned through the gates in detail and saw 20-25 people inside Lakshaya's compound. "First, let us get in," Arjun answered.

The boys looked at Arjun and slowly opened the gates to get in. Arjun stood and admired Lakshya. The distance from the gates to the main door was 400-500 feet. Lakshya stood tall and high in the centre of the huge garden protected by a compound, and 20 feet wide gate through which the boys got in. Arjun felt a vibe growing that he never experienced before.

"This is it." Arjun said, looking at the boys. "True that," Abhimanyu replied.

"Now or never," said Rishi. "Absolutely," Dhruv said.

Just when the boys walked towards the main door where Aarav and Vivaan stood, Arjun looked behind and saw a police van getting into Lakshya. The police Gypsy was parked next to the garden. Arjun noticed Vishnu driving his black Gypsy and parked next to the police Gypsy. Just as Vishnu stepped out, Arjun and Abhimanyu screamed, "DAD," and ran towards him, Rishi and Dhruv were behind them. People of the neighborhood now started gathering just outside Laksya to know the reason why cops entered Lakshya. Vivaan was shocked and didn't know what to do.

"Dad, what is all this??" Arjun asked. "Why are you and the cops here dad??" Abhimanyu asked in a surprised tone.

Rishi and Dhruv were right behind Arjun and Abhimanyu. Vishnu just smiled. "What the hell is happening?" Aarav questioned in anger, pointing at the cops.

The crowd was witnessing the mayhem, like the last over of a nail-biting cricket match. Arjun looked at the police officer and said to Abhimanyu, "Look, Abhi, it is dad's friend, ACP Justin uncle. Justin, a well-built man in his early 30s, walked towards Aarav and said, "You are under arrest for forgery. You forged the documents and claimed Lakshya to be yours. We did an investigation and found out that Lakshya has no legal heir. You are a fraud Mr. Aarav. You produced fake documents that said Lakshya was yours by illegally influencing big shots. You are charged with a non-bailable offense and hereby under arrest." Justin showed all the fake documents Aarav had made to prove Lakshya was his and the arrest warrant. Arjun was spellbound and did not know what to do.

"One of our missions is over??" Dhruv interrupted them. "Yes, one more to go." Vishnu gave a pathetic look towards Aarav. Rishi and Dhruv could not contain their thrill. Vivaan looked at Dad in a pathetic manner. Vivaan was told that Lakshya was legally owned by Aarav.

Vivaan always stood for truth, unlike his dad. Aarav stormed towards the gate in an attempt to escape. Justin noticed this and pulled Aarav into the police Gypsy... The cop moved the car. Vivaan followed in his car. The crowd left after the chaos was over.

The boys were the only one left in Lakshya. Arjun screamed in delight. Rishi and Dhruv hugged Abhimanyu. One out of two missions was complete. Arjun's delight turned into frown when he thought of the ring. "What do we do about the ring??" Arjun asked; the boys' sudden happiness turned into frown.

The boys ran inside Lakshya, "MAYA!!" screamed Arjun. The spirit appeared in front of them. The boys narrated the story one by one: "One mission is done; the ring will be with you soon," Maya said, turning towards Arjun. Arjun was about to say something when Maya interrupted "Oh, we have a company," she added.

Rishi and Dhruv looked behind; four hefty men barged through the main door with a petrol tanker to burn Lakshya down. It was Aarav's henchmen. Arjun ran out, and the others followed. Maya knew that she had the power to get into a person's soul for some time, but that person should be inside Lakshya.

Maya was restricted to use the power only once. Once, she enters a body, that body will not be able to sustain such power and will die when she leaves the body, and hence the owner of the body will die. Arjun and the others started to punch and kick with all their might. The goons were healthy and strong.

The kicks and punches were of no use. The boys were starting to get knocked to the ground. Arjun was in a fix. He and Abhimanyu were the only ones standing. He wanted to help Rishi and Dhruv who fell down. Abhimanyu ran to lift Rishi and Dhruv.

A goon followed Arjun. Arjun noticed that it was the leader of the goons. He ran behind the leader. Maya knew it was her turn to join the party. She vanished, and suddenly, the leader of the goon stopped and called the other three goons. The three came close to the leader and got punched and kicked by their own leader. Abhi, Rishi and Dhruv could not believe what they were watching. Arjun saw that Maya was missing from where she stood; he knew it was her spirit friend in business.

"It is MAYA." Arjun said. Abhimanyu, Rishi and Dhruv started to laugh as they watched their soul buddy smash the goons.

The boys were so engrossed in the event happening in front of them that they forgot that one goon ran from there and was behind Arjun with a rod. The goon hit Arjun on the head. Arjun fell to the ground. The other two goons were rubbing their respective bruises.

Abimanyu was in tears as Rishi and Dhruv chased the stabber. Maya ran towards Arjun, lifted her head and Screamed, "ARJUUN!!!"

He was motionless screamed Abhimanyu could not control his tears, Maya, in anger left the leader's body and the leader's body fell flat on the ground. The other goon's, didn't know what they were experiencing.

Maya went back as a soul screamed, "BOYSSS, HERE IT COMES." Rishi and Dhruv stopped. The goons kept running. Abhimanyu knew what was coming. He wiped his tears. The wind blew heavier. Abhimanyu, who was next to Arjun flew six feet away.

A blue light came from the sky and hit Arjun. The goons saw that the gate was on the other side, if they wanted to reach the gates, they had to cross the dramatic area. Arjun was on this knee, he felt like his body was possessed of immense power and energy.

The beautiful silver ring with a dark blue stone embarked in the centre was on his finger. He saw images of Sadvik, wearing the ring and the powerful metal vanished from Sachin's body like a dream. He shook his head as out of shock. Arjun stood up. Abhimanyu hugged Arjun.

Rishi and Dhruv ran toward Arjun in excitement. Arjun ran to the goon who stabbed him, and just one punch was enough to make the goon fly ten feet far, "SCRAAM!!" Arjun screamed in anger.

The other two goons picked up their leader's dead body and the other goons one by one and ran off.

"WE DID IT," Abhimanyu said.

"THE MISSION IS OVER," said Rishi, adding to the excitement.

"WOW! It is over," Dhruv said. The boys saw Arjun admiring the ring. They took a closer look at the ring. "MAYA..." Arjun said.

The boys searched everywhere in Lakshya, screaming her name. But their soul friend didn't appear in front of them. They were in tears. It was like the movies; a soul vanished right after their mission. "NOO..." Arjun screamed. "Is she gone forever??" Abhimanyu asked, wiping the tears off his face.

"She could have at least said bye," Rishi said emotionally.

Dhruv was lost for words. "We need to accept this; she might not... return since our mission is completed. Her soul is free." Arjun said with emotion. At that very moment,

Arjun got a call from Kalidas that Shalini met with an accident and is now in ICU. Arjun was in tears, and they all rushed to the city hospital. When they arrived near the ICU, Arjun and the boys saw Shalini's well-wishers were in agony. "She is critical; her vitals are sinking by the minute. We are trying our best, but our efforts have a limit," said a Doctor to Kalidas. "Is there no hope, Doctor?" Kalidas questioned. "I am sorry to say, but we are helpless; only a miracle can bring her back," Doctor replied. Kalidas was weeping; the boys surrounded Arjun to comfort him; Arjun took a deep breath and tried to console Kalidas. Arjun had tears running down as he consoled Kalidas. Abhimanyu and the others were tailing and comforting Arjun as Arjun stood there motionless. Right as the Doctor was walking away from Kalidas, a nurse screamed from Shalini's room, "Doctor, her pulse is nil; all her vitals have dropped."

The doctor opened the door to Shalini's room; the nurse inside saw the doctor and said in shock, "Her pulse is back to normal…"

The doctor closed the door and rushed towards Shalini.

Arjun, Kalidas and the others waited anxiously.

The Doctor stormed out after a few minutes and said to Kalidas, "A miracle has occurred. Shalini was gone, but the very next moment, Shalini was back with normal vitals. Shalini is recovering and is out of danger."

"All her vitals are fine. She can move to the room in a couple of days," Kalidas hugged Arjun in excitement.

After a couple of days, Arjun got a call from Kalidas.

"Arjun, Shalini is completely fine; she will be discharged today. She wants to talk to you. Can you please come?" Kalidas asked.

"That is so good to hear, uncle. I will reach there right away, Uncle," answered a relieved Arjun.

"She is in room number 126 on the first floor," Kalidas added.

"Ok, Uncle," Arjun said.

Arjun reached the room. Kalidas was walking towards Arjun, "Go in Arjun, I shall bring tea from the canteen," said Kalidas.

"Ok, Uncle," replied Arjun.

Arjun knocked on the door.

"Come in," Shalini said.

Arjun walked in and sat next to Shalini. Shalini held Arjun's hand and asked, "How is the ring?"

Arjun was shocked to hear this. "What??? How do you know… how…???"

Shalini interrupted Arjun and explained, "That day, when we were in Lakshya, you got the ring and trashed the goons away; that is when you received that call from Kalidas."

Arjun interrupted and said "Yeah, I remember a worried Kalidas uncle, informing about the accident; we rushed to the city hospital…"

"I also followed you to the hospital since the curse broke the moment you got the ring, that is when I heard the chief doctor saying that there is no hope to bring her back," she said.

"And then?" Arjun asked.

"I was very sad to hear the doctor saying helplessly that they couldn't do anything more, and only a miracle could save her. I thought of a plan that would make everyone happy and relieved. I immediately scanned her memory from her birth to that moment and entered her body as soon as her soul left," Shalini said.

"So, now you can talk and live like Shalini?" Arjun questioned.

"Yes, now, I can continue as Shalini for the rest of my life. But I need a promise from you; this must be kept as a secret between us forever." Shalini confirmed.

"I promise," Arjun assured and hugged her.

"Do you still have your memory as Maya?" Arjun questioned.

"I was Maya so the memory I have of Maya and Laya will stay in the corner of my mind. We were unable to live our life to the fullest in our past life, so let us live our life to the fullest together as one in this life," Shalini added.

Arjun smiled and said, "This life let us fulfil our dreams together."

After a few months, since Lakshya was a property with no legal heir, the government put Lakshya up for auction, and Vishnu was successful in purchasing Lakshya. Aarav was locked up in jail; Vivaan slowly forgot the past by working at Vishnu's friend's company in Kochi. Arjun and Abhimanyu, along with their parents and furry friend, Ricky, moved to Lakshya. Lakshya now looked like a beautiful mansion with new paint.

Arjun was watching Abhimanyu and his friends play cricket in Lakshya's huge yard.

"Arjun, Abhimanyu…" Vishnu called from inside the house.

Abhimanyu and Arjun ran inside.

"Sit down," Vishnu said.

Arjun and Abhimanyu sat next to Anjali. Ricky was playing with his favorite toy.

"Arjun, since you talked about fixing your alliance with Shalini after you guys get placed, Anjali and I had a chat with Kalidas, and he said that Shalini also talked to Kalidas about the alliance. He was planning to talk to us about that today, and he is completely ok with the proposal," Vishnu said.

Arjun jumped in excitement; Abhimanyu and Anjali hugged Arjun, and Vishnu also hugged them in happiness.

www.ingramcontent.com/pod-product-compliance
Lightning Source LLC
LaVergne TN
LVHW061602070526
838199LV00077B/7150